The Gateway to Storyland

11/2013

This Book Belongs
to Sophie & Mackenzie Golotzhober

God Bless You
Both

Love,

Mese Linda
+
Big Dave

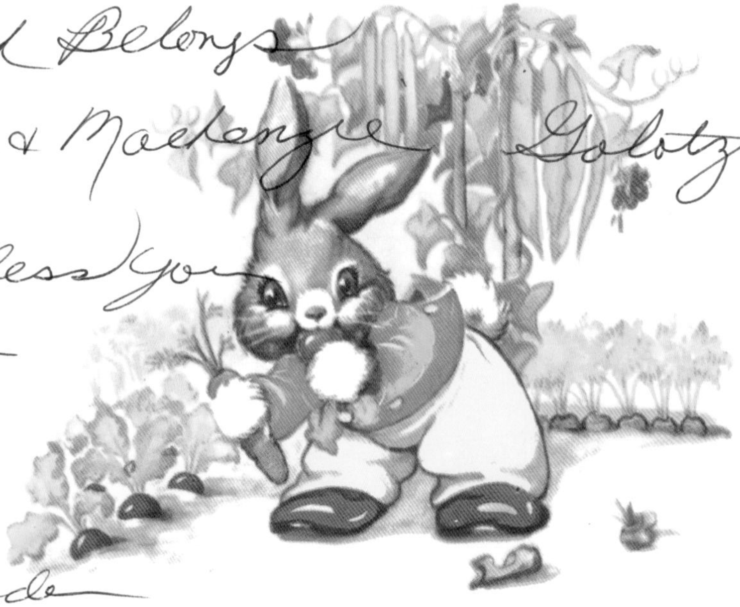

Favorite Nursery Stories and Poems

Edited by Watty Piper • Illustrated by Eulalie

BARNES
&NOBLE
BOOKS
NEW YORK

This edition published by Barnes & Noble, Inc.,
by arrangement with The Putnam & Grosset Group

1998 Barnes & Noble Books

ISBN 0-7607-0641-7

Printed and bound in China

98 99 00 01 02 03 M 9 8 7 6 5 4 3 2 1

Midas

"Who will take the wheat to the miller?" asked the Little Red Hen.

Contents

Once upon a time, there lived in a tiny house a little old woman and a little old man. They were very lonely, for they had no children of their own to fill their home with laughter and happy songs.

One day, while baking gingerbread, the little old woman said to herself out loud, "I will make a gingerbread boy." So she mixed the gingerbread dough and rolled it out with great care. With a round cookie cutter she then formed a head from the dough, and with her clever fingers she shaped a little round body with a pair of arms and two sturdy legs.

"And now for the clothes," she said, smiling to herself as she poured hot chocolate syrup over the gingerbread dough and smoothed it into a nice little jacket and a pair of trousers. With six fat raisins she made pretty buttons for his coat, and with pink sugar frosting she fashioned a little mouth. For his eyes she used two drops of frosting and for his nose a tiny lump of sugar.

But how she knew that this gingerbread dough, when nicely baked, would hop out of the oven, I cannot tell—unless, perhaps, a pretty fairy whispered to her in her dreams that such a wonderful thing would happen.

Then she placed the gingerbread boy on his back in the pan, put him in the oven, and closed the door. She swept and cleaned the house while waiting for him to bake glossy brown.

As the dough was baking, the little canary bird sang in her gilded cage:

"Fire burn and oven bake,
Turn the little ginger cake
Waiting in the shiny pan
To a little ginger man."

All of a sudden a little voice shouted from the oven:

"Open the door! Open the door!
I want to come out and play on the floor."

The little old woman knew at once that her dream had come true. She dropped her broom and ran happily to open the oven door. Out jumped the gingerbread boy to the floor of the kitchen.

His chocolate jacket fit so well,
If a tailor had made it, you could not tell.
His eyes shone like stars, for the frosting of white
Had stolen a gleam from the warm firelight,
And the smile of the little pink mouth made him seem,
To the little old woman, the child of her dream.

But, oh dear, dear! Instead of playing about in the neat little kitchen, the naughty little gingerbread boy ran out the open door, shouting at the top of his voice:

"A Gingerbread Boy, I am, I am!
I can run from you, I can, I can!"

"Stop, stop!" shouted the little old man in the garden, but the Gingerbread Boy paid no attention and slipped through the gate. He ran down the road as fast as his gingerbread legs would go, shouting at the top of his voice:

"A Gingerbread Boy, I am, I am!
I can run from you, I can, I can!"

By and by, he came to a field where some men were mowing the tall grass with long scythes.

"Stop, stop!" shouted the mowers on seeing the little Gingerbread Boy, but he only answered:

"A Gingerbread Boy, I am, I am!
I can run from you, I can, I can!
I ran away from a little old woman,
A little old man,
And now from *you* I can run,
I can!"

By and by, he came to a big red barn by the side of a hill. Looking through the open door, he saw the farmers threshing the wheat. "You can't catch me!" he shouted through the doorway. Then away he ran, looking back and crying:

"A Gingerbread Boy, I am, I am!
I can run from you, I can, I can!
I ran away from a little old woman,
A little old man,
A field full of mowers,
And now from *you* I can run, I can!"

And away he ran, faster than ever, without listening to the farmers' cries of "Stop, stop, little Gingerbread Boy!"

After a while he met a Red Cow with soft brown eyes.

"Stop, stop!" she called with a motherly moo. "I'll take you home to my spotted calf."

"Not unless you catch me," the Gingerbread Boy said boastfully, and he ran down the lane, almost bumping into a big fat pig with a little curly tail, who was looking through the old fence rail.

"Stop and play with me awhile,"
said the big fat Pig with a happy smile.
But the little Gingerbread Boy
Answered, "Catch me if you can!"

Running down the lane, he shouted:

"A Gingerbread Boy, I am, I am.
I can run away from you, I can!
I ran away from a little old woman,
A little old man,
A field full of mowers,
A barn full of threshers,
An old red cow,
And now from *you* I can run, I can!"

So on and on he ran, until at last he came to the end of the road.

Then he turned up a path through the shady wood,
Where close to a brook a little house stood.
But the Gingerbread Boy didn't know that within
Lived a terrible cat with sharp claws and a grin.

"Come in and have supper with me," said the sly old cat with a soft purr, as the tired little Gingerbread Boy rested on the front step of the house.

"Don't go in," whispered a little bird in the treetop. "That sly cat will eat you for supper!"

"Come in, come in," repeated the old cat, who was too deaf to hear the little bird's warning.

"Run home, run home, before it is too late!" chirped the little bird from the treetop. "The lonely old woman is anxiously waiting for you. Run home, run home—before it is too late!"

"Don't keep me waiting!" cried the cat quite suddenly. Growing impatient, she reached for the Gingerbread Boy with her terrible claws.

"Run, Run!" shouted the little bird. With a frightened cry the Gingerbread Boy jumped up and ran swiftly back through the woods to the roadway.

"Botheration!" said the sly old cat with a snarl. She turned back into her little house, saying:

"The Gingerbread Boy smelt ever so nice,
I would like to lick the chocolate ice.
His candy eyes, so round and sweet,
And his raisin buttons I'd like to eat."

On and on ran the little Gingerbread Boy, past the big fat Pig, who grunted kindly, "Hurry, hurry, hurry home!"

Past the motherly Red Cow, who softly mooed, "Hurry, hurry, hurry home!"

Past the barn full of threshers, who smiled and shouted, "Hurry, hurry, hurry home!"

Past the field where the mowers stopped their work to call out, "Hurry, hurry, hurry home!"

Past the little old man in the garden and right into the arms of the little old woman, who pressed him warmly to her heart and whispered, "Welcome home, my little Gingerbread Boy!"

Once upon a time there were three little kittens, and their names were Brownie, Blackie, and Snowball.

They lived with their mother in a pretty little cottage next to Farmer Brown's meadow.

All day long they would play very happily together, always sharing their toys and playthings.

One day Mamma Cat gave each of them a nice new pair of mittens.

Brownie's mittens were a beautiful red color.

Blackie's mittens were a lovely shade of green.

And Snowball's mittens were bright blue.

"Now, kittens, you may go out in the meadow and play, but be careful not to lose your mittens," said Mamma Cat.

So away ran Brownie, Blackie, and Snowball, as fast as their little legs could go.

Oh, they had a fine time playing hide-and-seek, skipping rope, and chasing the field mice in the meadow.

But their little paws soon became very warm, and they took off their new mittens and put them down in the field.

In a little while Mamma Cat called, "Come Brownie, Blackie, and Snowball. Dinner is ready."

So the three little kittens ran home quickly. When they got there, alas, it was clear that—

> The three little kittens, they lost their mittens,
> And they began to cry,
> "Oh Mummy dear, we sadly fear,
> Our mittens we have lost!"
> "What! Lost your mittens? You naughty kittens!
> Then you shall have no pie."
> Meow, meow. Meow, meow.

"Now, run straight back to where you were playing and find your mittens," said Mamma Cat.

The three little kittens hurried off and sure enough, right where they had left them—

The three little kittens, they found their mittens,
And they began to cry,
"Oh Mummy dear, see here, see here,
Our mittens we have found!"

"What! Found your mittens? You darling kittens!
Then you shall have some pie."
Purr, purr. Purr purr.

"Now, put on your mittens and come and eat," said Mamma Cat.

The three little kittens put on their mittens
And soon ate up the pie.
"Oh Mummy dear, we greatly fear
Our mittens we have soiled!"

"What! Soiled your mittens? You naughty kittens!"
Then they began to sigh.
Meow, meow. Meow, meow.

PURR·FECT
PUSSIES
SUPER
SOAP
PURR-
FECT
SUDS

Then Mamma Cat said to her three little kittens, "Now here is some soap. Go and wash your mittens right away, and try not to soil them again."

The three little kittens, they washed their mittens,
And hung them up to dry.
"Oh Mummy dear, look here, look here!
Our mittens we have washed!"

"What! Washed your mittens? You darling kittens!
But I smell a mouse close-by!
Hush, Hush! Meow, Meow!"
Meow, meow. Meow, meow.

MY SHADOW

I have a little shadow that goes in and out
with me,
And what can be the use of him is more
than I can see.
He is very, very like me from the heels up to
the head;
And I see him jump before me, when I jump
into my bed.

The funniest thing about him is the way
he likes to grow—
Not at all like proper children, which is
always very slow;
For he sometimes shoots up taller like
an India-rubber ball,
And he sometimes gets so little that there's none
of him at all.

He hasn't got a notion of how children ought
to play,
And can only make a fool of me in every sort
of way.
He stays so close beside me, he's a coward you
can see;
I'd think shame to stick to nursie as that shadow
sticks to me!

One morning, very early, before the sun was up,
I rose and found the shining dew on every
buttercup;
But my lazy little shadow, like an errant
sleepyhead,
Had stayed at home behind me and was fast asleep
in bed.

The Rooster, the Mouse and the Little Red Hen

A long time ago, a pretty little white house with green shutters stood on a hillside. In this little house lived A Rooster, A Mouse, and A Little Red Hen.

Across the valley, on a different hill, stood another little house. *This* little house was not well-kept. The windows were broken, the doors creaked, and the garden was full of weeds.

In this house lived A Wicked Fox and Four Bad Little Foxes.

Early one morning, the four little foxes went to their father and cried, "Oh Father, we are so hungry! We have not eaten for three whole days."

The big fox sat thinking a long time. Then, in a gruff voice, he said, "A Rooster, A Mouse, and A Little Red Hen live in the little white house on the hill across the valley..."

"They are nice and fat!" shouted the little foxes. "They would be good to eat!"

"Fine," said the big fox. "I'll take my gunnysack and go and catch The Rooster, The Mouse, and The Little Red Hen."

Then the four little foxes jumped for joy and shouted, "We will prepare the fire for our dinner!"

Away ran the big fox, until he reached the neat little white house on the other side of the valley.

He peeked through the window just as the Rooster and the Mouse came grumbling down into the kitchen, where the good Little Red Hen was bustling about, putting things in order. It was time to fix breakfast.

"Who will bring in the wood for the fire?" asked the Little Red Hen.

"I won't," answered the Rooster.

"Nor I," squeaked the lazy Mouse.

"Then I must do it myself," said the Little Red Hen, and off she went to the woodpile.

"Who will fill the kettle?" asked the Little Red Hen, when she was back in the kitchen.

"I won't," answered the lazy Rooster.

"Nor I," repeated the Mouse.

"Then I'll do it myself," answered the Little Red Hen, and off she hopped to the spring, carrying the big iron kettle.

"Now, who will cook the breakfast?" asked the Little Red Hen, when she returned.

"I won't," said the proud Rooster.

"Nor I," squeaked the lazy Mouse.

"Then I will do it myself," said the good Little Red Hen. And she did so at once.

All through the breakfast, the Rooster and the Mouse grumbled and grumbled, upsetting the milk and dropping crumbs on the floor.

"Now, who will wash the dishes?" asked the Little Red Hen, hoping that her friends would not be grumpy and cross after breakfast.

"I won't," answered the Rooster.

"Nor I," said the tired Mouse.

"Then I will do it myself," said the good Little Red Hen. Humming a little song, she soon had everything spick-and-span.

"Now, who will help me make the beds?" said the Little Red Hen.

"I won't" answered the Rooster.

"Nor I," repeated the Mouse.

"Then I will do it myself," and up the stairway went the Hen.

The lazy Rooster and Mouse found their comfortable chairs, and soon they were fast asleep.

When the bad fox saw the Rooster and the Mouse asleep, he knocked on the door:

Tap-tap-tap-tap.

"I wonder who that can be?" asked the sleepy Mouse.

"Why don't you look? answered the lazy Rooster.

"It must be the postman," said the Mouse, "and he may have a letter for me."

So, without making sure who was there, the Mouse opened the door, and in jumped the big, wicked fox.

The little Mouse screamed and tried to hide in the cupboard, while the frightened Rooster cried, "Cock-a-Doodle!" and jumped on the mantel.

But the wicked fox took the little Mouse by the tail and the Rooster by the neck and tossed them into his sack.

Hearing all the noise, the Little Red Hen came running down the stairs—right into the arms of the cunning fox. He popped her into the bag with The Rooster and The Mouse.

He took a long piece of string out of his pocket and tied it tightly around and around the sack.

Then he put the sack on his back, and down the hill he went.

As they were bumped about in the bag, the Rooster and the Mouse felt very, very sorry that they had been so cross and lazy.

They both began to cry, wondering what would happen to them.

"Cheer up," said the Little Red Hen. "It's never too late to change your ways. Look. I have my sewing kit with me, and soon you shall see what I am going to ask you to do."

By and by, Mr. Fox got very tired from carrying his heavy load and thought he would rest a while. So, when he came to a shady tree, he dropped his sack on the ground and sat down beside it.

Soon he was fast asleep, dreaming of what a fine dinner he and the four greedy little foxes would have when he reached home.

When the Little Red Hen heard the fox snoring, she opened her work bag and took out a little pair of scissors, a needle and thread, and a small thimble.

The fox did not hear her and kept on snoring.

Quick as a wink, she cut a hole just large enough for the Mouse to creep through.

"Run!" she whispered to the Mouse. "Run as fast as you can, and bring back a stone as large as you can carry."

While the Mouse was dragging back a stone as big as himself, the Little Red Hen snipped away at the hole until it was large enough for the Rooster to get through.

"Run!" she whispered to the Rooster. "Run as fast as you can, and bring back a stone as large as you can carry."

The Rooster soon came back with a stone as big as himself, and he and the Mouse carefully pushed their stones into the sack.

Then the Little Red Hen jumped out of the sack. She, too, found a stone as big as herself and pushed it into the sack.

Taking out her needle and thread, the Hen put on her thimble and sewed up the hole as quickly as she could.

Then all three ran home, happy to get away from the bad fox.

They shut and bolted the door hurriedly, closed the windows, and drew in 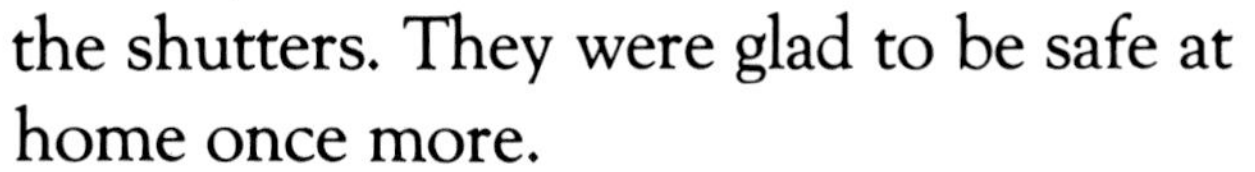
the shutters. They were glad to be safe at home once more.

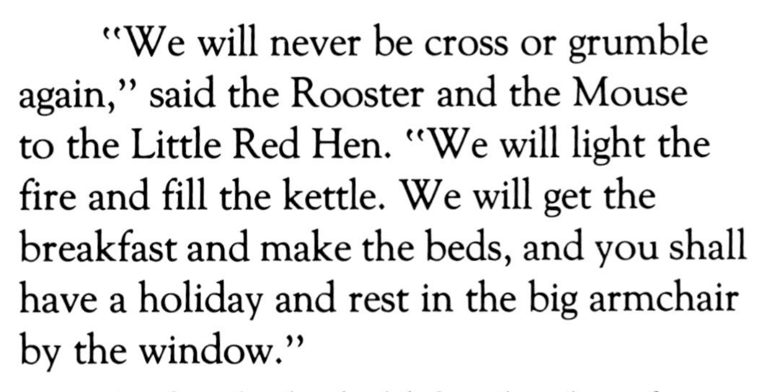
"We will never be cross or grumble again," said the Rooster and the Mouse to the Little Red Hen. "We will light the fire and fill the kettle. We will get the breakfast and make the beds, and you shall have a holiday and rest in the big armchair by the window."

As for the bad old fox, he slept for a long, long time.

When he woke up, he rubbed his sleepy eyes and shouldered his sack, grumbling and saying, "I have overslept, and I must hurry home."

So the bad fox took a shortcut home, a path that ran through the meadows and across a stream.

When he was crossing the stream, his foot slipped, and—*Splash!*—the sack dropped into the water.

The fox tried to grab the sack, but the heavy stones quickly sank it to the bottom.

"Dear, dear," he said with a sigh. "There goes our dinner," and he went home with nothing for the four greedy little foxes, who had to go to bed without any supper.

And to this day, the Big Fox and the Four Little Foxes have never found out that The Rooster, The Mouse, and The Little Red Hen still live happily together in the pretty white house on the other side of the valley.

One fine April morning, while doing her spring housecleaning, Mrs. Pig suddenly looked up, and said, "O deary dear! I do believe there is nothing in the house for supper!"

She pushed her dust cap back over one ear, stumbled over the mop, and went tap-tapping to see if there was anything in the icebox. But, alas, all she found to feed her husband and her three little pigs were two leaves of lettuce and one egg.

Poor Mrs. Pig. She was an old-fashioned woman who always wanted to be the perfect housewife, but just then the piano and all the chairs were in the middle of the room. The rug sat rolled up in one corner, and the scrub bucket was full of the foamiest suds. Mrs. Pig was wearing an old dress, and an apron, and big, clumsy shoes to keep her toenails pretty. She couldn't go to the market that way!

Just then, Mr. Pig, who was an old-fashioned husband, looked cautiously into the room. He had been hiding, because he knew Mrs. Pig was often not in a good mood when there was spring-cleaning going on.

"Mrs. Pig, I could go to the market for you," he said.

Mrs. Pig picked up her mop and said, "But Mr. Pig, what do you know about shopping?"

"Nothing," said Mr. Pig. "But I do know what I like."

"Well, all right," said Mrs. Pig, "but buy something that can be cooked in one pot. I won't have time to fix a big supper."

So Mr. Pig put on his yellow trousers, his green striped coat, and his red necktie and started through the forest to the market. The birds were singing, little breezes were blowing, and flowers were blooming everywhere. Mr. Pig did a little scamper and a little prance as he went along happily. Shopping was certainly more fun than being around housecleaning.

Soon he came to the big market. First he went to the vegetable side of the shop.

"Good morning, Mr. Pig," said the vegetable man. "Did Mrs. Pig send a shopping list with you?"

"No," said Mr. Pig importantly. "I'm doing the shopping myself today."

The vegetable man laughed. Here was a chance to get rid of the wilted spinach he hadn't been able to sell the day before!

"Here is something nice," he said, showing Mr. Pig the old spinach.

"Well," said Mr. Pig, "I don't know much about vegetables, but I know what I like. And, I *don't* like that spinach!"

So the vegetable man brought out some long, fresh, golden carrots, small new red potatoes, and pretty bunches of white spring onions.

"Aha!" said Mr. Pig. "That's more to my liking! But first I must go to the meat market and see what I can buy to go with the vegetables. Mrs. Pig said all the supper must cook in one pot, because it's spring-cleaning day."

So Mr. Pig went to the meat man.

"Good morning, Mr. Pig," said the meat man. "Let me see Mrs. Pig's shopping list."

"Good morning," said Mr. Pig, "I don't have a list. I'm doing the shopping myself today. What meat do you have that's nice and tasty?"

"Well," said the meat man, "here are some fine pork chops."

Mr. Pig shuddered.

"Or some hamburger that's very fine."

"No," said Mr. Pig. "I don't know much about meat, but I know what I like, and that isn't it."

"Well," said the meat man, "I have some nice shoulder of lamb. The very best spring lamb."

Mr. Pig thought of the golden carrots, the little red potatoes, and the small white onions. Then he thought of the lamb shoulder.

"My, oh my!" he said. "That sounds like good lamb stew. Give me ten pounds."

So the meat man wrapped up the meat, and Mr. Pig scurried to the vegetable man as fast as a very fat pig can scurry. He bought five pounds of potatoes, five bunches of carrots, and three bunches of onions. His basket was a little heavy, but he didn't mind because he was so excited at the thought of the fine dinner he and his family would have.

Mr. Pig was so caught up in his thoughts as he hurried home that he almost stumbled over Mr. Possum.

"Hi there, Mr. Pig!" shouted Mr. Possum. "Where have you been this fine spring morning?"

"To market, to market," said Mr. Pig merrily.

"Not to buy a fat pig, I imagine!" said Mr. Possum, who was a little tactless.

"Dear me, no," said Mr. Pig. "I've ten pounds of lamb, and onions, potatoes, and carrots. Mrs. Pig will make us a fine dish for supper tonight."

"Yum yum!" said Mr. Possum. "There's just nothing like lamb stew." And his mouth began to water as he thought of the fine dinner.

Mr. Pig was feeling so good that he loved all the world, so he said, "Well, come over to our house for supper tonight at seven-thirty."

"Lamb stew!" said Mr. Possum excitedly. "I'll be there."

Mr. Pig didn't know what Mrs. Pig would say about company for supper on housecleaning day, and he began to worry a little. He shifted his heavy basket to his other arm and went on slowly.

"Hi, Mr. Pig," came a voice from overhead.

Mr. Pig looked up, and there was Mr. Squirrel on the branch of an oak tree. "Is Mrs. Pig sick?" asked the squirrel.

"No," said Mr. Pig, "She's cleaning house. I don't know much about shopping, but I do know what I like, and it's lamb stew. That's what I've got here. Or at least the makings of a lamb stew."

"Oh my, oh my!" said Mr. Squirrel. "Next to acorns, I like lamb stew best. Especially, at this time of the year."

"Well," said Mr. Pig. "There's going to be a lot of lamb stew at our house at seven-thirty. Come along and we'll give you some."

"I'll be there," said Mr. Squirrel. "I'll certainly be there."

Mr. Pig shifted the basket back to his other arm. Then he stopped to pick a large bunch of buttercups and some violets growing along the path. He thought Mrs. Pig might feel better about company for supper on housecleaning day if he brought her a present. He put the flowers carefully on top of the onions and looked up to see Mr. Dog coming along the path.

"Hi, Mr. Pig," said Mr. Dog. "I haven't seen you for many a moon. Where's Mrs. Pig?"

"She's at home doing the spring-cleaning," said Mr. Pig. "I don't know anything about cleaning, but I know what I don't like, and it's mops and pails and soapsuds. So, I went shopping until the house is straight again."

"Shopping, eh?" said Mr. Dog. "As a matter of fact, Mrs. Dog has gone to visit her family for a few days, and I'm down to my last bone. What did you buy in the market?"

PIGGY
PHOTO
ALBUM
A.B.C

"Well, I've a fine lamb stew here for Mrs. Pig to cook. A good deal of meat, long golden carrots, little green spring onions, and—"

Mr. Pig stopped when he saw Mr. Dog's mouth watering and a big tear beginning to trickle out of one eye.

"See here," said Mr. Pig. "Why don't you come to our house at seven-thirty and have supper with us?"

"Well," said Mr. Dog eagerly, "I'm taking care of our three puppies while Mrs. Dog is away, and I don't have anyone to leave them with."

Mr. Pig stopped and picked three daffodils. "Puppies don't eat much," he said.

Mr. Dog waited.

"Mrs. Pig likes puppies," he said.

Mr. Dog waited some more.

"Tell you what, Mr. Dog. You bring the puppies along, and they can eat at the side table with our three little pigs."

"Thank you, Mr. Pig!" said Mr. Dog. "We'll be there."

Mr. Pig went on slowly. Every now and then he stopped to pick more buttercups and violets. He was worrying a good deal about what Mrs. Pig would say when he told her how many were coming for dinner on cleaning day.

When he finally got home, the house was shining. The rug was back on the floor. The pail and mop and broom were back in the cupboard. Mrs. Pig was dressed in a pretty checkered dress with a green turban around her head. Housecleaning had not taken as much time as she had feared.

Mr. Pig handed her the flowers and put the market basket on the kitchen table.

"My my, Mr. Pig!" said Mrs. Pig. "These flowers are very pretty, and you've picked me a big bunch."

"Well," said Mr. Pig, "I don't know much about flowers, but I know what I like, and it's buttercups and violets. They are just right for spring. Like lamb stew." He stopped a minute. "And company in a clean house."

Mrs. Pig didn't seem to hear him. She was busy unwrapping bundles.

"My my, Mr. Pig! What a lot of meat! We'll never eat all this!"

"Well, Mrs. Pig," said Mr. Pig slowly. "It's a good thing I did get a lot, because on my way home I met Mr. Possum and Mr. Squirrel, and I invited them to dinner. Then I met Mr. Dog, whose wife is out of town, and I invited him because he was down to his last bone. He had no one to leave the puppies with, so I told him the puppies could eat with our three little pigs. They're all coming to supper tonight at seven-thirty." Then Mr. Pig held his breath and waited for Mrs. Pig to get angry.

But Mrs. Pig was not angry. "I finished the housecleaning in record time today," she said. "I think company for supper is a good idea." And she took her biggest kettle, newly shined and polished. She chopped meat and scrubbed carrots and scraped potatoes and peeled onions and made a pot of lamb stew so full it came right up to the brim.

And then she scrubbed the three little pigs.

And then she scrubbed Mr. Pig.

And... at seven-thirty all the animals came and sat down with the Pig family. They each ate more than one helping, and all the guests said it was the most wonderful stew thay had ever eaten.

That night, when Mr. Pig latched the door to their clean house, he hugged his plump, round wife and said, "Well, Mrs. Pig, I don't know much about women, but I *do* know what I like!"

There was once a man who owned a little gray pony. Every morning, when the dewdrops were still on the pink clover and the birds were singing their morning song, the man would jump on his pony and ride away, *clippety, clippety, clip!*

The pony's four small hoofs played the jolliest tune imaginable on the smooth, paved road. The pony's head was always high in the air, and his two little ears were always perked up, for he was a merry gray pony and loved to go *clippety, clippety, clop!*

The man rode everywhere on the pony, to town and to country, to church and to market, uphill and downhill. One day while he was riding he heard something fall with a clang onto the road. Looking back, he saw a horseshoe lying there. And when he saw it, he cried out:

"What shall I do? What shall I do
If my little gray pony has lost a shoe?"

Then down he jumped in a great hurry and looked at one of the pony's forefeet, but nothing was wrong. He lifted the other forefoot, but the shoe was still on that foot, too. He examined one of the hind feet and began to think that the horseshoe on the road did not belong to his pony. However, when he looked at the last foot, he cried again:

"What shall I do? What shall I do?
My little gray pony has lost a shoe!"

Then he made haste to go to the blacksmith, and when he saw the smith, he called out to him:

> "Blacksmith! Blacksmith! I come to you,
> For my little gray pony has lost a shoe!"

But the blacksmith answered:

> "How can I shoe your pony's feet
> Without any coal for me to heat?"

The man was downcast when he heard this, but he left his little gray pony in the blacksmith's care and hurried here and there to find coal.

First he went to the store. When he got there he said:

> "Storekeeper! Storekeeper! I come to you;
> My little gray pony has lost a shoe!
> And I have to find some coal to heat,
> So the blacksmith can shoe my pony's feet!"

But the storekeeper answered:

> "Well, I have apples and candy to sell,
> And more nice things than I can tell;
> But I have no coal for you to heat,
> So the blacksmith can shoe your pony's feet!"

Then the owner of the pony went away sighing and saying:

"What shall I do? What shall I do?
My little gray pony has lost a shoe!"

By and by he met a farmer coming to town with a wagon full of supplies, and he said:

"Farmer! Farmer! I come to you;
My little gray pony has lost a shoe!
And I have to find some coal to heat,
So the blacksmith can shoe my pony's feet."

Then the farmer answered:

"I've bushels of corn and hay and wheat,
I've lots of food for your pony to eat;
But I have no coal for you to heat,
So the blacksmith can shoe your pony's feet."

So the farmer drove away and left the man standing in the road sighing and saying:

"What shall I do? What shall I do?
My little gray pony has lost a shoe!"

In the farmer's wagon the man saw corn, which made him think of the mill, so he hastened to the mill and called to the dusty miller:

"Miller! Miller! I come to you;
My little gray pony has lost a shoe,
And I have to find some coal to heat,
So the blacksmith can shoe my pony's feet!"

The miller came to the door in surprise, and when he heard what was needed, he said:

"I have wheels that go round and round,
And stones to turn till the grain is ground;
But I have no coal for you to heat,
So the blacksmith can shoe your pony's feet!"

Then the man turned away sadly and sat down on a rock near the roadside, sighing and saying:

"What shall I do? What shall I do?
My little gray pony has lost a shoe!"

After a while a very old woman came down the road, driving a flock of geese to market. When she came near the man, she stopped to ask him his trouble. He told her about it, and when she had heard it all, she laughed till her geese joined in with a cackle. Then she said:

"Surely you know where coal is found!
You must go to the miner who works in the ground!"

Then the man sprang to his feet, thanked the old woman, and ran to the miner. Now the miner had been working hard down in the mine, which was under the ground where it was so dark that he had to wear a lamp on the front of his cap to help him see his work. He had plenty of black coal and gave great lumps of it to the man, who took them in haste to the blacksmith.

The blacksmith made a great red fire and hammered out not one but *four* fine new shoes, with a *cling!* and a *clang!* and fastened them on with a *rap!* and a *tap!* Then away rode the man on his little gray pony—*clippety, clippety, clap!*

ONE STORMY NIGHT

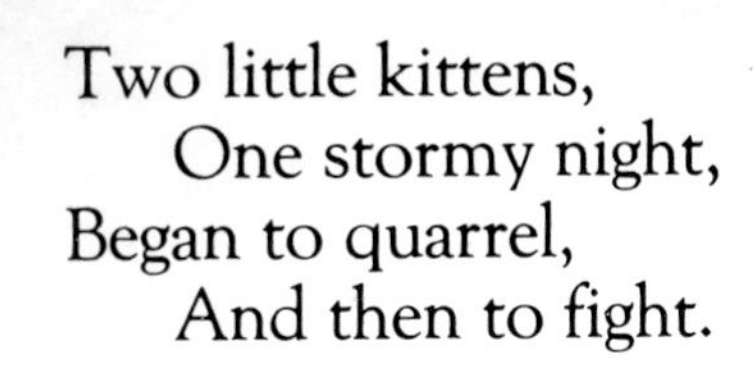

Two little kittens,
 One stormy night,
Began to quarrel,
 And then to fight.

One had a mouse,
 The other had none;
And thus the quarrel
 Had just begun.

"*I'll* have that mouse,"
 Said the first little cat.
"*You'll* have that mouse?
 We'll see about that!"

"I *will* have that mouse,"
 Said cat number one.
"*You won't!*" said the other,
 His bow all undone.

The noisy cats
And the little mouse
Were suddenly swept
Right out of the house.

The ground was covered
With layers of snow,
And the two little kittens
Had nowhere to go.

The shivering kittens
Argued no more,
And finally someone
Opened the door.

The kittens crept in,
As quiet as mice,
All wet with snow
And cold as the ice,

And found it much better,
On that stormy night,
To lie by the fire
Than quarrel and fight.

Once upon a time, in a tiny house with a pebbly roof and a little stone chimney, there lived a young chicken named Chicken Little.

One day as Chicken Little was scratching in her garden, a pebble fell off the roof and hit her on the head.

"Oh, dear me!" she cried. "The sky is falling! I must go and tell the king." And away she ran down the road.

By and by she met Henny Penny, who was going to the store. "Where are you going?" asked Henny Penny.

"I'm going to tell the king the sky is falling," answered Chicken Little.

"How do you know the sky is falling?" asked Henny Penny.

"Because a piece of it fell on my head!" said Chicken Little.

"May I go with you?" begged Henny Penny.

"Certainly," answered Chicken Little, and she hastened on, followed by Henny Penny.

Turning up a shady lane they met Ducky Daddles.

"Where are you two going?" asked Ducky Daddles.

"We are going to tell the king the sky is falling," answered Henny Penny.

"How do you know?" asked Ducky Daddles.

"Chicken Little told me," said Henny Penny.

"A piece of it fell on my head!" cried Chicken Little.

"May I go with you?" asked Ducky Daddles.

"Certainly," answered Chicken Little, and away went Chicken Little, Henny Penny, and Ducky Daddles.

By and by they passed the farmyard where Goosie Poosie was talking to Piggy Wiggy. When Goosie Poosie saw them hurrying by she asked, "Where are you three going?"

"The sky is falling and we are going to tell the king," answered Ducky Daddles.

"How do you know?" asked Goosie Poosie.

"Chicken Little told me," said Henny Penny.

"A piece of it fell on my head!" cried Chicken Little.

"May I go with you?" asked Goosie Poosie.

"Certainly," said Chicken Little, so they all started off again.

By and by, whom should they meet but Turkey Lurkey, who had just been talking to Bunny Rabbit.

"Where are you four going?" asked Turkey Lurkey.

"The sky is falling and we are going to tell the king," answered Goosie Poosie.

"How do you know?" asked Turkey Lurkey.

"Ducky Daddles told me" said Goosie Poosie.

"Henny Penny told me," said Ducky Daddles.

"Chicken Little told me" said Henny Penny.

"A piece of it fell on my head!" cried Chicken Little.

"May I go with you?" asked Turkey Lurkey.

"Certainly," said Chicken Little.

Then Turkey Lurkey followed Chicken Little, Henny Penny, Ducky Daddles, and Goosie Poosie. On and on they went, along the road that led to the castle of the king.

But someone else saw them as they went along. It was Foxy Loxy, and he came creeping through the woods after them. As he followed them, he thought about what a fine meal each of them would make. Suddenly Foxy Loxy jumped out from behind the bushes and said, "Where are you all going?"

"Why, Foxy Loxy, don't you know the sky is falling?" they all replied at once. "We are going to tell the king."

"How do you know?" asked Foxy Loxy.

"Goosie Poosie told me," said Turkey Lurkey.

"Ducky Daddles told me," said Goosie Poosie.

"Henny Penny told me," said Ducky Daddles.

"Chicken Little told me," said Henny Penny.

"A piece of it fell on my head!" cried Chicken Little.

"I know a shortcut to the palace," said Foxy Loxy. "Shall I show it to you?"

"Oh, certainly," they all answered at once.

Foxy Loxy led them along until they reached the door of his house.

"This is the short way to the king's palace. You'll get there more quickly if you follow me. I will go in first and call you one at a time, as the passage is very narrow," said Foxy Loxy.

Then he called Turkey Lurkey, who came in and closed the door. Foxy Loxy caught him by the neck. Just as he was about to put Turkey Lurkey into the pot, Turkey Lurkey flew up in the air and out the window. Home he ran as fast as he could go.

Then Foxy Loxy called Goosie Poosie, who came in and closed the door. Foxy Loxy caught her by the neck. But just as he was about to put her into the pot, Goosie Poosie flew up in the air and out the window. Home she ran as fast as she could go.

Next Foxy Loxy called Ducky Daddles, who came in and closed the door. Foxy Loxy caught her by the neck. But just as he was about to put her into the pot, Ducky Daddles flew up in the air and out the window. Home she ran as fast as she could go.

Then Foxy Loxy called Henny Penny, who came in and closed the door.

Foxy Loxy caught her by the neck. But just as he was about to put her into the pot, Henny Penny flew up in the air and out of the window. Home she ran as fast as she could go.

When Chicken Little saw Turkey Lurkey, Goosie Poosie, Ducky Daddles, and Henny Penny flying out the window and running home, she became worried. She knew Foxy Loxy was up to some mischief.

When a little chicken is worried, she scratches her head. When Chicken Little scratched her head, she felt something hard buried in her feathers. She pulled it out and looked at it. It was the pebble which had fallen off the roof.

"How silly I am," she said. "This is not a piece of the sky, just a pebble off my roof. In fact, I don't think the sky can fall at all."

Then home went Chicken Little, feeling quite happy. And to this day she has never worried about the sky falling again.

Once upon a time, long, long ago, there lived an old Mother Pig who had three little pigs. Mother Pig was very poor and could not keep her piggies at home any longer.

So one day, with tears in her eyes, she said to all of them, "Little Piggies, you are nearly grown. You must go out into the world now and each build your own little house to live in."

So the three little pigs started out to make their own way in the world.

They walked and walked, till they came to a point where the road branched off in three directions. One little pig took the road to the right. One little pig took the road to the left. And the third little pig walked straight down the middle road.

The first little pig had not gone very far when he met a man carrying a bundle of straw.

"Please, Mr. Man," said the little pig, "may I have some straw? I want to build a house."

The man felt sorry for the little pig, so he gave him some straw. Then the little pig built a house.

The very next day, along came a big, bad wolf and knocked at the door of the first little pig.

"Hello, Little Pig!" he called. "Let me come in. I want to speak to you."

"No, no. Not by the hair of my chinny, chin, chin. I won't let you in," said the little pig. "I can hear you from where you are."

Then the wolf growled, "Little Pig, you let me in, or I'll huff and I'll puff till I blow your house down!"

But the little pig would not let him in.

So the wolf huffed and puffed—till he blew the house down, and the little pig ran away.

The second little pig met a man with some wood.

"Please, Mr. Man," said he, "may I have that wood? I want to build a house."

The kind man gave him the wood, and the little pig built his house.

When night came, the little pig went to bed.

Soon, the big, bad wolf came along and rapped at the door, and the little pig got up and went to the window.

"Hello, Little Pig!" the wolf called. "Let me come in."

"No, no. Not by the hair of my chinny, chin, chin. I won't let you in."

"Then," said the wolf, "I'll huff and I'll puff till I blow your house down!"

But the little pig still would not let him come into the house.

So the wolf huffed and puffed till he blew the house down, but the little pig ran away so fast that the wolf could not catch him.

Now the third little pig walked along the road till he met a man with some bricks and mortar.

"Please, Mr. Man," said he, "may I have some bricks and mortar? I want to build a house."

The man gave him the bricks and mortar, and the third pig built himself a strong little house with a nice green door, large windows, and a bright red roof.

The next day, who should come along but the big, bad wolf. He knew it was the house of the third little pig and he knocked on the door.

The little pig looked out of the upstairs window and asked the wolf what he wanted.

"Hello, Little Pig," said the wolf. "Let me come in."

"No, I will not let you in," said the pig. "Go away!"

"You had better let me in, Little Pig," said the wolf, "or I'll huff and I'll puff till I blow your house down."

"No, no. Not by the hair of my chinny, chin, chin. I won't let you in," said the little pig.

So the wolf huffed and puffed and puffed some more, but the strong little house would not blow down. He took another big breath and huffed and puffed, but still he could not blow the house down.

When he found that all his huffing and puffing did no good, he tried to think of some way to get the little pig out of his house.

"Do you like turnips, Little Pig?" asked the wolf. "I know where there is a fine field full of them."

"Where, where?" asked the little pig.

"Why, down in Farmer Brown's field. Let us go and get some."

"What time are you going?" asked the little pig.

"I'll come for you at six o'clock tomorrow morning," answered the wolf.

"That's fine," said the little pig. "I'll be ready."

But he got up at five o'clock the next morning and was back home before six with a potful of fine turnips.

When the wolf came at six o'clock and knocked at the door, the little pig called out, "Why, I found the field and already have some turnips for dinner."

Of course the wolf was very angry. Then he tried to think of another way to fool the little pig.

"Little Pig," said he, "I know where we can get some fine apples. Come with me tomorrow morning at five o'clock, and I will show you where they are."

"I'll be ready," said the little pig. He knew that the apples were down in Farmer Brown's orchard. He had seen them on his way to get the turnips. So the wise little pig went to the orchard at four o'clock the next morning.

He was about to climb down from a tree with a basket full of apples when who should come along but the big, bad wolf.

"Hello, Little Pig," the wolf called up to him. "I see you got here before me."

My, but the little pig was frightened.

"Are they sweet apples?" asked the wolf.

"Yes, very nice and sweet," said the little pig. "I'll throw one down to you." He threw the apple as far from the tree as he could. The wolf ran to pick it up, and the little pig jumped down and ran home as fast as his little legs could go. He locked the door of his house behind him, and the big, bad wolf did not catch him that day.

The next day the wolf came again. "Little Pig," said he, "there is going to be a fair in town today. Don't you want to go?"

"Yes, I do!" said the little pig. "What time will you be ready?"

"I'll be ready at three, and we'll go together," said the wolf.

But the little pig went early, as usual, and had a jolly time seeing the sights and riding on the merry-go-round.

He happened to buy a big butter churn and was taking it home when he saw the wolf coming up the hill. He had to hide before the wolf saw him, so he climbed inside the churn. The churn fell over on its side and rolled down the hill with the little pig in it. Faster and faster it went.

When the wolf suddenly saw the big strange object rolling down on him, he was dreadfully frightened. He turned and ran as fast as his legs could carry him, completely forgetting about the fair and the third little pig.

The little pig rolled home safely and lived happily ever after.

Have you ever heard of the Sugarplum Tree?
'Tis a marvel of great renown!
It blooms on the shore of the Lollipop sea
In the garden of Shut-Eye Town;
The fruit that it bears is so wondrously sweet
(As those who have tasted it say)
That good little children have only to eat
Of that fruit to be happy next day.

When you've got to the tree, you would have
a hard time
To capture the fruit which I sing;
The tree is so tall that no person could climb
To the boughs where the sugarplums swing!
But up in that tree sits a chocolate cat,
And a gingerbread dog prowls below—
And this is the way you contrive to get at
Those sugarplums tempting you so:

You say but the word to that gingerbread dog
And he barks with such terrible zest
That the chocolate cat is at once all agog,
As her swelling proportions attest.
And the chocolate cat goes cavorting around
From this leafy limb unto that,
And the sugarplums tumble, of course, to the ground,
Hurrah for that chocolate cat!

There are marshmallows, gumdrops, and peppermint canes,
With stripings of scarlet or gold,
And you carry away of the treasure that rains
As much as your apron can hold!
So come, little child, cuddle closer to me
In your dainty white nightcap and gown,
And I'll rock you away to that Sugarplum Tree
In the garden of Shut-Eye Town.

The Little Red Hen and the Grain of Wheat

Once upon a time, a Little Red Hen and her brood of fluffy little chicks lived in a little farmyard.

One day the Little Red Hen sighed and said, "Dear, oh dear. I must not forget that when winter comes the green meadows and fields will be covered with snow. Then we cannot scratch for food. I must see that our little cupboard is filled with good things to eat before winter comes." Then she bustled about her little house to make it neat and clean.

When the breakfast dishes were washed and the beds made, she put on a pretty bonnet and gathered her little ones.

"Come, my little chicks," she clucked. "We must find some grains of wheat." Then she hunted all around until at last she found some grains in a pile of chaff in the barnyard. These she picked up and put into her apron.

"Now, who will help me sow the wheat?" asked the Little Red Hen, looking around at her barnyard neighbors.

"Not I," quacked the Duck.

"Not I," squeaked the Mouse.

"Not I," grunted the Pig.

"Then I'll sow it myself," answered the Little Red Hen, as she scratched and scratched in the earth until she had made a nice little garden in which to plant the yellow seeds.

It was not an easy task to sow all the grains of wheat and cover them over with fresh earth. The Little Red Hen was very tired by sundown, but—

The happy feeling in her heart
Told her she had done her part.

Gathering her little chicks, she led them home to the small house under the apple tree where they lived.

Soon the sunshine and the rain helped all the golden grain to sprout, and by the time fall came the wheat was strong and tall enough to be harvested.

One sunny autumn day, the Little Red Hen started out by herself, leaving her chicks to play in the neat little house. Up the shady lane she hurried to the farmyard.

"Now who will help me cut the wheat?" she asked her neighbors.

"Not I," quacked the Duck.

"Not I," squeaked the Mouse.

"Not I," grunted the Pig.

"Then I will cut it myself," said the Little Red Hen, and she bustled into the barn to find a sickle. After she found it, she set to work. When the wheat was all cut, it was time to go home to her little chicks. Down the shady lane she hurried to get supper for them.

Bright and early the next morning, she again hurried off to the farmyard—to thresh the wheat. "Cluck, cluck, cluckerty cluck. It's time to thresh the wheat. Who will help me beat each grain from the chaff?" asked the Little Red Hen.

"Not I," quacked the Duck.

"Not I," squeaked the Mouse.

"Not I," grunted the Pig.

"Then I'll thresh it myself," answered the Little Red Hen, and with a smooth round stick, she beat the wheat from the stalks.

"There," she said. "Now that's done." Gathering all the little grains into a big round pile, she asked, "Who will help me carry the wheat to the windmill?"

"Not I," quacked the Duck.

"Not I," squeaked the Mouse.

"Not I," grunted the Pig.

"Then I'll carry it myself," answered the Little Red Hen. Bustling into the big red barn, she hunted around until she found an empty sack.

As soon as she had filled it with the grains of wheat, she placed it in a little wheelbarrow and set off down the road to the mill.

There in the doorway stood Rusty Dusty Miller, his hat and coat white with flour dust. "Good morning, Little Red Hen," said Rusty Dusty Miller, taking off his dusty cap politely. "What have you in the sack?"

"Wheat which I have sown for bread, kind sir," said the Little Red Hen.

"Then I will grind it for you," answered Rusty Dusty Miller. Lifting the sack out of the little wheelbarrow, he carried the wheat into the mill and ground it into nice, smooth flour. Then he filled the sack with the flour and placed it in the wheelbarrow. The Little Red Hen went home singing merrily:

"I've sowed and reaped
And walked to the mill.
I've carried this sack
Up and downhill.
Now we must bake
To have our fill."

"Who will help me bake the bread?" asked the little Red Hen, when she reached the farmyard.

"Not I," quacked the Duck.

"Not I," squeaked the Mouse.

"Not I," grunted the Pig.

"Then I will make it all myself," answered the Little Red Hen. When it was baked, the Little Red Hen clucked happily:

"The bread is baked both light and sweet.
Now who will come and help me eat?"

"I will," quacked the Duck, waddling through the doorway.

"I will," squeaked the Mouse, peeking out of the cupboard.

"I will," grunted the Pig, looking through the window.

"No, you won't," answered the Little Red Hen. "I sowed the seeds, reaped the wheat, threshed the grain, carried it to the mill and back again, kneaded the dough, and baked the bread. Cluck, cluck. Come, my little chicks. I made this bread for you, not for lazy folks."

"Dear me," quacked the Duck. "Why didn't I help the Little Red Hen?"

"Dear me," squeaked the Mouse. "I'm sorry I was so selfish."

"Dear me," grunted the Pig. "I was too lazy to help the Little Red Hen, so now I must go hungry."

"Eat, my little chicks. You were too small to do the hard work," said the Little Red Hen. "But, as for the rest of you—

Lazy folks must hungry go,
If they do not help to sow.
If they do not help to reap,
They'll be hungry and they'll weep.
If they do not bake the bread,
Lazy folks shall not be fed.
Eat your fill, my chickies, do.
I have made it just for you."

The Tale of Peter Rabbit

Once upon a time there were four little Rabbits, and their names were

Flopsy,

Mopsy,

Cotton-tail,

and Peter.

They lived with their Mother in a sandbank, underneath the root of a very big fir tree.

"Now, my dears," said old Mrs. Rabbit one morning, "you may go into the fields or down the lane, but don't go into Mr. McGregor's garden. Your father had an accident there; he was put in a pie by Mrs. McGregor."

"Now run along, and don't get into mischief. I am going out."

Then old Mrs. Rabbit took a basket and her umbrella, and went through the wood to the baker's. She bought a loaf of brown bread and five currant buns.

Flopsy, Mopsy, and Cotton-tail, who were good little bunnies, went down the lane to gather blackberries.

But Peter, who was very naughty, ran straight away to Mr. McGregor's garden and squeezed under the gate!

First he ate some lettuces and some French beans; and then he ate some radishes.

And then, feeling rather sick, he went to look for some parsley.

But around the end of a cucumber frame, whom should he meet but Mr. McGregor!

Mr. McGregor was on his hands and knees planting out young cabbages, but he jumped up and ran after Peter, waving a rake and calling out "Stop thief!"

Peter was most dreadfully frightened; he rushed all over the garden, for he had forgotten the way back to the gate.

He lost one of his shoes among the cabbages, and the other shoe amongst the potatoes.

After losing them, he ran on four legs and went faster, so that I think he might have got away altogether if he had not unfortunately run into a gooseberry net, and got caught by the large buttons on his jacket. It was a blue jacket with brass buttons, quite new.

Peter gave himself up for lost, and shed big tears; but his sobs were overheard by some friendly sparrows who flew to him in great excitement, and implored him to exert himself.

Mr. McGregor came up with a sieve, which he intended to pop upon the top of Peter; but Peter wriggled out just in time, leaving his jacket behind him.

He rushed into the tool-shed, and jumped into a can. It would have been a beautiful thing to hide in, if it had not had so much water in it.

Mr. McGregor was quite sure that Peter was somewhere in the toolshed, perhaps hidden underneath a flowerpot. He began to turn them over carefully, looking under each. Presently Peter sneezed—"*Kertchoo!*" Mr. McGregor was after him in no time, and tried to put his foot upon Peter, who jumped out of a window, upsetting three plants. The window was too small for Mr. McGregor, and he was tired of running after Peter. He went back to his work.

Peter sat down to rest; he was out of breath and trembling with fright, and he had not the least idea which way to go. Also he was very damp from sitting in that can.

After a time he began to wander about, going lippity—lippity—not very fast, and looking all around.

He found a door in a wall; but it was locked, and there was no room for a fat little rabbit to squeeze underneath.

An old mouse was running in and out over the stone doorstep, carrying peas and beans to her family in the wood. Peter asked her the way to the gate, but she had such a large pea in her mouth that she could not answer. She only shook her head at him. Peter began to cry.

Then he tried to find his way straight across the garden, but he became more and more puzzled. Presently, he came to a pond where Mr. McGregor filled his watering cans. A white cat was staring at some goldfish; she sat very, very still, but now and then the tip of her tail twitched as if it were alive. Peter thought it best to go away without speaking to her; he had heard about cats from his cousin, little Benjamin Bunny.

He went back towards the toolshed, but suddenly, quite close to him, he heard the noise of a hoe—*scr-r-itch, scratch, scratch, scritch.* Peter scuttered underneath the bushes. But presently, as nothing happened, he came out, and climbed upon a wheelbarrow, and peeped over. The first thing he saw was Mr. McGregor hoeing onions. His back was turned toward Peter, and beyond him was the gate!

Peter got down very quietly off the wheelbarrow and started running as fast as he could go along a straight walk behind some black-currant bushes.

Mr. McGregor caught sight of him at the corner, but Peter did not care. He slipped underneath the gate, and was safe at last in the wood outside the garden.

Mr. McGregor hung up the little jacket and the shoes for a scarecrow to frighten the blackbirds.

Peter never stopped running or looked behind him till he got home to the big fir tree.

He was so tired that he flopped down upon the nice soft sand on the floor of the rabbit hole, and shut his eyes.

His mother was busy cooking; she wondered what he had done with his clothes. It was the second little jacket and pair of shoes that Peter had lost in a fortnight!

I am sorry to say that Peter was not very well during the evening.

His mother put him to bed and made some camomile tea; and she gave a dose of it to Peter! "One tablespoonful to

be

taken

at

bedtime."

But Flopsy, Mopsy, and Cotton-tail had bread and milk and blackberries for supper.